CYNTHIA RYLANT

POPPLETON

BOOK ONE

Illustrated by
MARK TEAGUE

SCHOLASTIC INC.
New York Toronto London Auckland Sydney

For Robert Martin Staenberg
and his lucky parents
C. R.

To Parker and Tammy and Michealla
M. T.

ISBN 0-590-84783-X

Text copyright © 1997 by Cynthia Rylant.
Illustrations copyright © 1997 by Mark Teague.
All rights reserved. Published by Scholastic Inc.

12 11 10 9 8 7 6 5 4 3   9   8 9/9 0 1 2/0

Printed in the U.S.A.   23

Designed by Kathleen Westray.

CONTENTS

NEIGHBORS

Poppleton used to be a city pig.

He did city things.

He took taxis.

He jogged in the park.

He went to museums.

Then one day Poppleton
got tired of city life.
He moved to a small house
in a small town.

Poppleton's small house
was charming.
It had a little sunroom
where Poppleton took naps.

It had lots and lots of shelves
where Poppleton kept things.
It had a little garden
where Poppleton planted corn.

And it had Cherry Sue.
Cherry Sue was Poppleton's
new neighbor.

Cherry Sue was very friendly.
In the mornings she called out,
"Yoo-hoo! Poppleton! Would you
like some oatmeal?"
So Poppleton had oatmeal
with Cherry Sue.

In the afternoons she called out,
"Yoo-hoo! Poppleton! Would you
like a toasted cheese?"
So Poppleton had toasted cheese
with Cherry Sue.

At night she called out,
"Yoo-hoo! Poppleton! Would you
like spaghetti?"
So Poppleton had spaghetti
with Cherry Sue.

This went on day after day.

At first it was fun.

But not for long.

Some mornings Poppleton did not want oatmeal.

He wanted to sleep.

Some afternoons Poppleton did not
want toasted cheese.

He wanted TV.

Some nights Poppleton did not
want spaghetti.

He wanted to practice
playing his harmonica.

But Cherry Sue kept calling,
"Yoo-hoo! Poppleton!"

One day when he was watering his lawn,
Poppleton couldn't take it anymore.
When Cherry Sue stuck her head out
the window and yelled "Yoo-hoo!"
Poppleton soaked her with the hose.
"Poppleton!" cried Cherry Sue, dripping.

Poppleton felt awful.

He ran to get a towel for Cherry Sue.

"I'm sorry, Cherry Sue,"
said Poppleton.

"I just got so sick of toasted cheese
and spaghetti and oatmeal.
Sometimes I just like to be alone."

"You too?" said Cherry Sue.
"I kept inviting you over because
I didn't know how to *stop* inviting
you over," she said. "I thought
it might hurt your feelings."

Then Poppleton soaked *himself*
with the hose.
They laughed and laughed.
Poppleton and Cherry Sue were
best friends from then on.

THE LIBRARY

Poppleton went to the library
every Monday.
Monday was *always* Poppleton's
library day.

If Cherry Sue invited him to
tea on Monday, Poppleton would say,
"Sorry. Library day."

If there was a wonderful parade
in town on Monday, Poppleton would say,
"Too bad. Library day."
Poppleton took library day
very seriously.

At the library Poppleton always got
a table all to himself.
He spread out each of his things
on the table:
his eyeglasses, his tissues,
his lip balm, his pocket watch,
his book marker, and his duffel.
Then he began to read.

Poppleton liked adventure stories.
He buried his head in an adventure book
every Monday, and left it there
all day long.

Sometimes he needed
a tissue for a sad part.

Sometimes he needed
lip balm for a dry part.

Sometimes he needed
his pocket watch for a slow part.
But he loved his adventure.

At the end of the day, Poppleton
finished the story.
He thanked the librarian
and packed up his things in his duffel.

Then he slowly walked home,
all dreamy from so much adventure.
Monday was Poppleton's
favorite day of all.

THE PILL

Poppleton's friend Fillmore
was sick in bed.
Poppleton brought Fillmore
some chicken soup.

"I feel terrible, Poppleton,"
said Fillmore.

"Have a bowl of soup," said Poppleton.

"First I have to take my pill,"
said Fillmore.

"Where is it?" asked Poppleton.

"Over there on the table," said Fillmore.

Poppleton brought Fillmore his pill.

"I can't take it like that," said Fillmore.

"You have to hide it."

"Hide it?" asked Poppleton.

"You have to hide it in my food,"
said Fillmore.

"I'll put it in the soup," said Poppleton.
"No, it has to be in something sweet,"
said Fillmore.
"Sweet?" asked Poppleton.

"Sweet and soft," said Fillmore.

"Sweet and soft?" asked Poppleton.

"Sweet and soft with raspberry filling," said Fillmore.

"Sweet and soft with raspberry filling?"
asked Poppleton.

"And chocolate on top," said Fillmore.

"Chocolate on . . . Fillmore, are you
talking about Cherry Sue's
Heavenly Cake?" asked Poppleton.

Fillmore smiled.

Poppleton went away.

Soon he came back with Cherry Sue's
Heavenly Cake.

"Now I can hide your pill,"
said Poppleton.

"Don't tell me which piece of cake
it's in," said Fillmore.

Poppleton sliced the cake into ten pieces.

He hid Fillmore's pill in one of them.

Fillmore had the first piece.

"Yum," said Fillmore.

"Did I take my pill?"

Poppleton shook his head.

Fillmore had another piece.

"Yum," said Fillmore. "Did I take it?"

Poppleton shook his head.

Fillmore ate piece after piece after piece.

"Did I take it?"

Poppleton kept shaking his head.

Finally there was only one piece

of cake left.

"Thank goodness," said Poppleton.

Fillmore looked at the piece of cake.

"I can't eat that one," he said.

"It has a pill."

"WELL, WHAT CAN YOU EAT?" shouted
Poppleton.

"Something lemony," said Fillmore. "With
coconut."

"I feel sick," said Poppleton. "Move over."

Poppleton and Fillmore were sick in bed
for three days.
They took *lots* of pills.
It took twenty-seven cakes
to get them down.

E
Ryl

$10⁻